Hershel the Jewish Reindeer

Written by
JEFF GELLER

Hershel the Jewish Reindeer, Published November, 2016

Cover and Interior Illustrations: Randy Jennings
Interior Layout: Howard Johnson
Editorial and Proofreading: Annamaria Farbizio, Ashley Fedor
Author Illustration by Joseph Gemellaro

Published by SDP Publishing, an imprint of SDP Publishing Solutions, LLC.

SDP Publishing
Permissions Department
PO Box 26, East Bridgewater, MA 02333
or email your request to info@SDPPublishing.com.

ISBN-13 (print): 978-0-9977224-2-0
ISBN-13 (ebook): 978-0-9977224-3-7

Printed in the United States of America

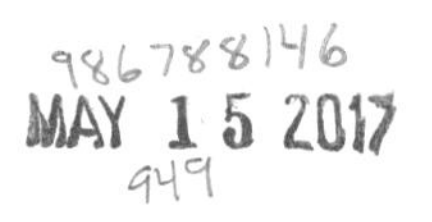

This story is dedicated
to my family: Susan,
Lily, Asa, and Will.

I would like to acknowledge
my mother Gloria for her
contributions and ideas,
my father Harold for his
support, and my sister Linda
for her creativity.

’Twas the day before Christmas and it soon would be night,

As the reindeer prepared for their holiday flight.

Delivering toys to good children should have made them real glad,

But leaving their own families at home made them feel sad.

Hershel, the Jewish reindeer, saw the tears in their eyes.

And he wondered, "Would it matter to Santa which one of us flies?

Chanukah is two weeks early this year,

Maybe I can help my friends with their holiday cheer."

HAPPY CHANUKAH

"But I can't pull this heavy sleigh all by myself."

To form a team, he called Sanchali, the Hindu elf.

When Sanchali learned how fast and far they would roam,

She said, "Let's ask Aalam for help, he's a Muslim Gnome."

Aalam said, "I know a reindeer who can float in the air,

Dawa is Buddhist, but Santa won't care.

In his life before this one, he was a bird,

He'd be happy to help us, just say the word."

PEACE

Then another reindeer stepped out from the mist,

"Hi, my name is Larry and I'm atheist.

That just means that I don't pray,

But I still can help the others by pulling this sleigh."

Hubert said, "I'm agnostic, which means I have doubt,
But that doesn't mean that I won't help you out.
I have many more friends who can help you to fly.
They have different beliefs—Taoist, Shintoist, Bahá'í."

Hershel watched as his team formed with glee,

As he thought, “If given the chance they would do this for me.”

He’d found stand-ins for Dasher, Comet, and Donner,

Flying for them would be quite an honor!

And Vixen, Blitzen, and Rudolph said grace,

Saying prayers for those who flew in their place.

Prancer and Cupid were swapped out with a bit of good luck,

"But who will guide the team?" Now Hershel felt stuck.

The important spot left was the one for Dancer.
Then the tooth fairy called Hershel with a helpful answer.
"This isn't my normal job, but I'll come right away,
I like working nights and can help guide this sleigh."

Santa came soon with his toy sack and gear,
"Let's make this a good run. It's just once a year.
On Hershel, on Sanchali, on Dawa," Santa said,
As they all buckled down and pulled on the sled.

"On Aalam, on Hubert," Santa called, "HO, HO, HO!"

But the sleigh was too heavy, and it just wouldn't go!

They counted the reindeer, gnome, elf, and fairy,

And someone called out, "What about Larry?"

“I’m sorry I’m late. Let’s get this sleigh in the air,”

“It’s just that my children want toys too! They say it’s not fair.”

Larry asked, “Can we give them some presents though they don’t believe?”

Santa said, “If they’ve been good I will check up my sleeve.”

With that Larry added a little more force,

And the sleigh lifted off and charted its course.

Everyone was happy to help one another,

Despite our differences, we are sisters and brothers!

About the Author

Jeff Geller, MD is part of a family that includes both the Jewish and Christian religious backgrounds. Storytelling became a favorite way to answer his children's endless questions: *Why does Dad always work on Christmas? Why do we have to go to school on Chanukah but not Christmas?* and *Can we get presents for BOTH Christmas and Chanukah?* 'Hershel' and other stories have helped his family embrace the most meaningful parts of the many traditions in his community.

Hershel the Jewish Reindeer

Jeff Geller

Author website: www.GellerBooks.com

Publisher: SDP Publishing

Also available in ebook format

Available at all major bookstores

www.SDPPublishing.com

Contact us at: info@SDPPublishing.com

CPSIA information can be obtained
at www.ICGtesting.com
Printed in the USA
LVOW05s1431030417
529438LV00022B/330/P

9 780997 722420